THE LITTLE GREEN MONSTER CLEANS UP THE BEACH

By ALISON INCHES

Illustrated by VIVIANA GAROFOLI

LITTLE SIMON • An imprint of Simon & Schuster Children's Publishing Division
New York London Toronto Sydney • 1230 Avenue of the Americas, New York, New York 10020
 • For information about special discounts for bulk purchases, please contact Simon & Schuster Special Sales at 1-866-506-1949 or business@simonandschuster.com.
The Simon & Schuster Speakers Bureau can bring authors to your live event. For more information or to book an event contact the Simon & Schuster Speakers Bureau at 1-866-248-3049 or visit our website at www.simonspeakers.com.
Manufactured in the United States of America • 1209 LAK • First Edition 2 4 6 8 10 9 7 5 3 1 • ISBN 978-1-4169-9514-2

Max the Little Green Monster loved the ocean! He loved to have picnics on the beach. He loved to play in the water.

"COWABUNGA!" shouted Max.

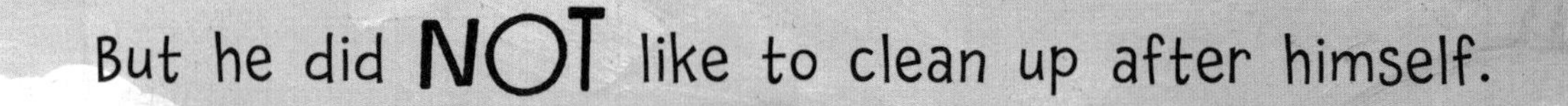

But he did **NOT** like to clean up after himself.

Max went to explore the tide pools and snorkeled along the coral reef. He wanted to see fish, sea stars, and bright pink coral.

But all he saw
was an empty BOTTLE,
a PLASTIC BAG,
an OLD TIRE,
and a
BROKEN TOY.

"Trash makes the ocean look ugly," said Max.

"I'll pick up the
trash on the beach so
it can't come
into the water!"

Max cleaned up the trash from his picnic
and he cleaned up other people's trash too.

He found so much litter that it filled the trash and recycling bins to their very tops.

"Now that's a lot of trash!" said Max the Little Green Monster. "I'll find out where it came from and stop it!"

He saw
beachgoers leave
their trash
on the beach.

"NO LITTERING!" said Max.

He saw boaters fling their trash overboard.
“The ocean **ISN’T** a trash bin!” said Max.

On the way home Max saw a painter rinse paint from his brushes into the gutter. . . .

A boy's balloon popped and he dropped it in the gutter. . . .
A girl with a new toy threw her plastic bag in the gutter. . . .

A group of kids playing on the street shot their ball right into a storm drain at the end of the gutter.

"WOW," said Max.
"Everything that falls
into the gutter
flows into the storm drain.

And everything in the storm drain empties into the ocean."

That means car oil, soapsuds, and
waste go into the ocean too, thought Max.

"Pollution at home is
bad for the ocean, too,"
Max said.

"I'll find out how to start
saving the ocean even when I'm away from it!"

Max learned that chemicals and soaps can poison sea plants . . .

fish can get stuck in trash . . .

sea turtles and birds can mistake things like plastic bags and balloons for food . . .

and birds and other ocean animals that get covered in oil can't stay warm or move around.

"WOW," said Max.
"I need to help
save the ocean!"

Now, Max keeps trash
from washing away in the
gutter by sweeping
the driveway with a broom
instead of using a hose.

He uses reusable
bags so that plastic
bags won't end
up in the ocean.

He drinks from a reusable water bottle so that plastic bottles won't hurt the animals.

He uses biodegradable sunscreen so that the chemicals won't pollute the ocean water.

He always picks up his trash and any other litter he might find.

And best of all, Max the Little Green Monster teaches his friends how to be green monsters.

KEEP THE OCEAN BEAUTIFUL

You can be a little green monster, too, and help save the ocean!